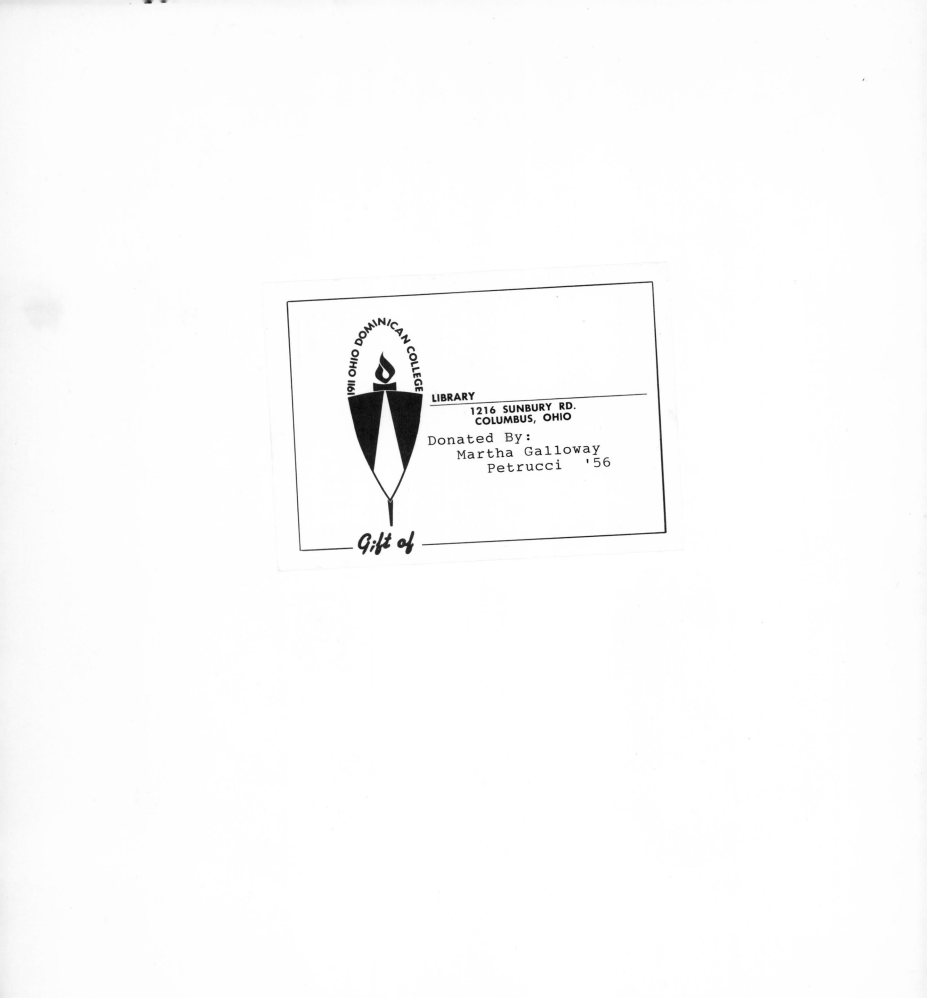

Walter Grieder

The Great Feast

For Alain

PARENTS' MAGAZINE PRESS: NEW YORK

Copyright © 1968 by Parents' Magazine Press
Printed in the United States of America
Library of Congress Catalog Card Number: 68-21079

Originally published in German as DAS GROSSE FEST
©1966 by Verlag Herder KG Freiburg, Germany

The cock crows.
The sun rolls up over the hills.
He rises and glides
like a ball of pure gold,
and the clouds are his wings.
The flowers tremble
in the early breeze.
In the trees the birds
begin their morning songs.
The day awakes.
It is the day of the Great Feast!
It is the day
of Violetta's wedding.

In the kitchen
everything is ready.
The pots and pans,
the mugs and jugs,
are clean and shining,
ready, side by side,
for the feast.
The water is steaming
in the kettle,
the logs are glowing
in the stove.
Flora the cook is grinding
coffee in the coffee mill.
Her eyes sparkle with joy.
Lumpi, the naughty dog,
sneaks to the basket
to see what he can find.
He keeps an eye on Flora
who must not catch him.
But Flora only smiles.
It is Violetta's wedding day.
Let him have his sausage.

Babette and Nanette
are awake already
and standing by the window.
Such a parade is going by!
Guests coming
with wonderful gifts,
the farmers bringing
delicious fruits and gay flowers,
and the baker with the
wonderful wedding cake!
Such confusion!
The chickens squawk
and fly out of the way.

What a way to take a bath!
Waves splash over the tub.
The floor, the walls
—even the ceiling
is getting a bath today.
The twins don't like to wash.
It's more fun to just play
in the water.
But today is the Great Feast.
Everybody must be clean.

Now which one is the
most beautiful?
"I am!" cries Babette.
"No, I am!" cries Nanette.
How quarrelsome the twins are.
"Hush!" says Mother.
"Today the bride is the
most beautiful.
But don't fret.
Both of you may carry her train."

The wedding ceremony is over.
The bride and bridegroom
leave the church
for the wedding dinner.
And there are the twins
right behind.
There is no fighting now.
They are as changed
as if they were suddenly
two angels on earth.

Down in the wine cellar
it is cool and damp.
The mice are playing and the cat
is trying to catch them.
He gets very angry when they
run away and hide in corners.
The cellar is a very
mysterious place,
but the light from the lamp
and the smell of ripe apples
make you feel braver.
Gustav is choosing the wine
for the dinner.
It must be the very best
because this is Violetta's
wedding day.
He tries it and says,
"This is fine."

The father raises his glass
and says, "Blessed be
the bride and groom."
Everybody is so pleased
and happy
except the two little girls.
They are impatient
because Flora is taking
too long
to bring the wedding cake.

Now the sun is high in the sky.
The ducks are quacking happily
on the pond,
and the bees are busy flying
from flower to flower.
The guests have come
into the garden
to walk along the paths
and look at the flowers.
A pheasant goes by,
showing his beautiful feathers
to everyone.
Babette runs quickly
to catch him
but the pheasant scoots off,
fast as a rabbit.

The girls decide to run away
from the party.
They go up to the attic
to play wedding.
"No one will bother
about our noise up here,"
says Nanette.
They open an old trunk
and take out beautiful clothes.
They dress up like a prince
and princess.
"Now we are a bride
and groom!" they cry.
Lumpi doesn't know who
they are, and he barks loudly.

Suddenly lovely music comes
from the drawing room.
Everyone is singing
a happy wedding song,
while a band plays
on brass horns.
The children are polite
and solemn
except for two naughty boys.

At last the ball begins.
Round and round go the dancers
and the ladies' dresses swish
behind them.
Such glowing cheeks
and sparkling eyes!
As the violins play
the children hop about
and laugh with joy.
Babette tries to make
Lumpi dance a waltz with her.
Grandmother sits quietly by,
watching it all.
She has a dreamy smile
as she remembers
her own wedding day.

Oh! Ah! Now it is dark
and see what is happening
in the garden.
The fireworks shoot into the sky
and burst with a crack and a boom
into huge flower blossoms
in the night.
It is very exciting.
The girls run quickly
from their friend Tino.
He is disguised as a donkey
and he is trying to scare them.

Nanette and Babette
are too excited
by what has happened all day.
They can't think of going
to sleep.
They are running and jumping
like wild animals
all over their bedroom.
But here comes Flora.
She claps her hands sharply.
"To bed you go now.
The Great Feast is over."

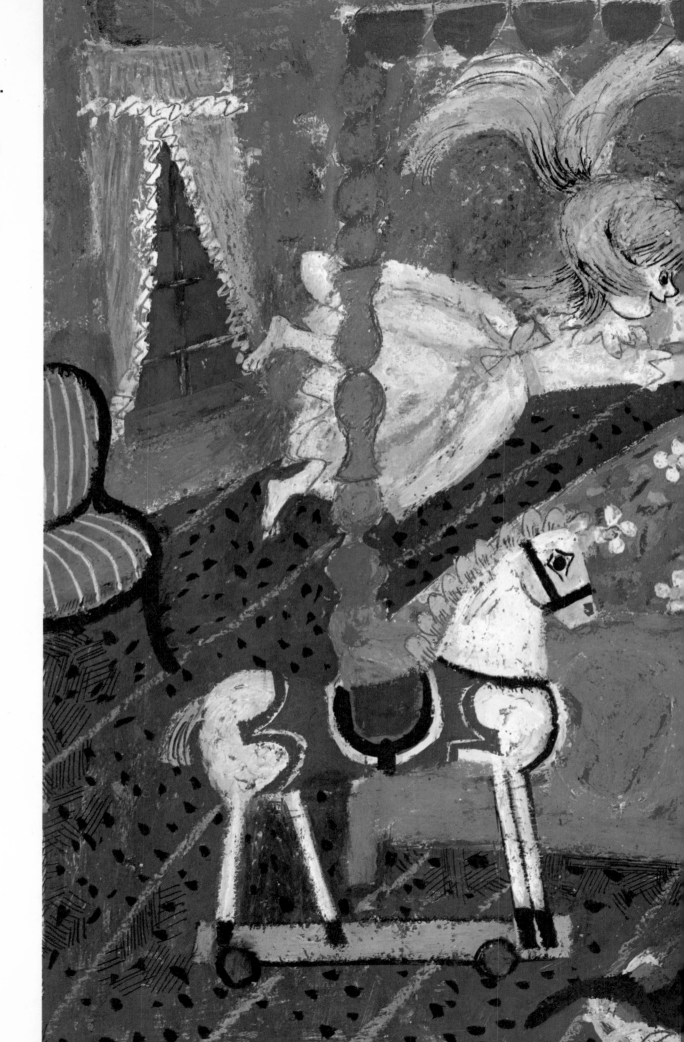

Everyone is at last asleep
and the house is dark.
In the night only foxes
and cats are about, prowling
in the shadows.
An owl sits in his tree
watching for a mouse
to scurry by.
And the yellow moon smiles down
on the world of night,
happy to see that all is well.

WALTER GRIEDER is one of the foremost writers and illustrators of children's books in Europe today. Born in Basel, Switzerland, he spent an adventurous childhood among circus performers in France. He returned to art school in Basel and set up a one-man studio there in 1956. He has also studied in Paris and London. The spirit and style of Mr. Grieder's work is closely bound up with his own personality. He does not accept manuscripts from publishers, but prefers to write his own stories, thus achieving a unity of art and text. His most recent books published in Europe include A VISIT TO A FACTORY and THE CARNIVAL. His PIERROT has also been published in the United States.